The Magic
Rainbow Smoothie

by Liza Charlesworth

ISBN: 978-1-338-89049-5

Designer: Cynthia Ng; Illustrated by John Lund

1 2 3 4 5 6 7 8 9 10   68   31 30 29 28 27 26 25 24 23 22

Printed in Jiaxing, China. First printing, January 2023.

It was a super-warm day in Troll Town.
So May decided to make a smoothie.
She had ice, milk, and a big blender.
But there was a problem.
She didn't have any fruit.

May's friends DID have fruit.
But there was a problem.
They didn't like to share.
But May had come up with a clever plan.
She only needed to stand beside her blender...
and wait.

After a while, her friend Stan
walked by with fresh strawberries.
"What are you making?" asked Stan.
"A magic rainbow smoothie!" replied May.
"How can a smoothie be magic?" asked Stan.

"Share your strawberries with me
and you will see," replied May.
So, Stan dropped them into the blender.
Plunk, plunk, plunk.
"Thanks! It will be ready soon," said May.

After a while, her friend Omar
walked by with fresh oranges.
"What are you making?" asked Omar.
"A magic rainbow smoothie!" replied May.
"How can a smoothie be magic?" asked Omar.

"Share your oranges with me
and you will see," replied May.
So, Omar dropped them into the blender.
Plunk, plunk, plunk.
"Thanks! It will be ready soon," said May.

After a while, her friend Linda
walked by with fresh lemons.
"What are you making?" asked Linda.
"A magic rainbow smoothie!" replied May.
"How can a smoothie be magic?" asked Linda.

"Share your lemons with me
and you will see," replied May.
So, Linda dropped them into the blender.
Plunk, plunk, plunk.
"Thanks! It will be ready soon," said May.

After a while, May's friend Luke
came by with some limes.
And Blake came by with some blueberries.
And Grace came by with some grapes.

They also wanted to know how
a smoothie could be magic.
So they dropped their fruit into the blender.
Plunk, plunk, plunk.

Now, May's blender was filled to the brim
with strawberries and oranges and lemons
and limes and blueberries and grapes.
May added ice cubes.
May poured in milk.

May put a lid on the blender.
Then, she pushed the button
to turn it ON.
Whizz, whizz, whizz!
Whirr, whirr, whirr!

A minute later, May pushed the button
to turn the blender OFF.
The magic rainbow smoothies were ready.
They were red and orange and yellow
and green and blue and purple!

May gave each of her friends a tall glass.
MMMMMMMMMMMMMMMMMM!
They all agreed their drinks were quite delicious.
But everyone had the same question:
"What makes these smoothies magic?"

"Hee, hee!" said May with a chuckle,
"These rainbow smoothies are magic
because they taught you how to share!"
After that, everyone in Troll Town
lived AND shared happily ever after.